For Coleen Salley

PUFFIN BOOKS
Published by the Penguin Group
Viking Penguin, a division of Penguin Books USA Inc.,
40 West 23rd Street, New York, New York 10010, U.S.A.
Penguin Books Ltd, 27 Wrights Lane, London W8 5TZ, England
Penguin Books Australia Ltd, Ringwood, Victoria, Australia
Penguin Books Canada Ltd, 2801 John Street, Markham, Ontario, Canada L3R 1B4
Penguin Books (N.Z.) Ltd, 182–190 Wairau Road, Auckland 10, New Zealand

Penguin Books Ltd, Registered Offices; Harmondsworth, Middlesex, England

First published in the United States of America by Viking Penguin,
a division of Penguin Books USA Inc., 1987
Published in Picture Puffins 1989
10 9 8 7 6 5 4 3 2
Copyright © James Marshall, 1987
All rights reserved

LIBRARY OF CONGRESS CATALOGING-IN-PUBLICATION DATA
Marshall, James, 1942–
The cut-ups cut loose / by James Marshall.   p. cm.
Summary: At the end of summer Spud and Joe eagerly return to
school for more practical jokes, unaware that Principal Lamer J.
Spurgle is out of retirement and awaiting them.
ISBN 0-14-050672-1
[1. Behavior—Fiction. 2. Schools—Fiction. 3. Humorous stories.] I. Title.
[PZ7.M35672Cv 1989]   [E]—dc19   89-30215

Printed in Japan by Dai Nippon Printing Co. Ltd.
Set in Aster

Spud Jenkins and Joe Turner were headed back to school.

Their mothers were beside themselves with joy.

Being the mother of a cut-up wasn't easy.

And Spud and Joe were a couple of *real* cut-ups.

They had gotten off to an early start.

And they had never stopped.

Cutting up was certainly challenging work.

But school was the biggest challenge of all.

"This year we'll really cut loose!" said Spud.

"You said it!" said Joe.

At the bus stop, they double-checked their supplies:

Two rubber rattlesnakes, five rolls of caps,
three boxes of premade spitballs,
a half-dozen stink bombs, and Joe's pet tarantula,
Intrepid.

"That should just about do it,"
said Spud.
Just then, they heard a loud car radio.

"Wow!" said Joe.
"Will you look at that!"
"It's that nice Mary Frances Hooley,"
said Spud.

Mary Frances Hooley and her little brother, James, were on their way to school at St. Bridget's across town.

"You souped up your car!" said Joe.

"Let us drive it!" said Spud.

"Oh please!!"

"Later, boys," said Mary Frances.
"I can't be late for school."
And off she roared.

"I'm glad we don't go to St. Bridget's," said Joe.
"Did you see all those books?"
"Those kids have it really rough," said Spud.

On the bus, some kids were talking.

"The new principal doesn't like kids," someone said.

"His name is Lamar Spurgle."

"Lamar *J.* Spurgle?" cried Joe.

They had already had one run-in with Spurgle,

and they didn't want another.

When the bus arrived at school,
Spud and Joe were the last to get off.
They had drastically changed their appearance.

"Maybe he won't recognize us," said Joe.
"Uh-oh," said Spud.
"Look who's standing at the top of the steps."

It was Lamar J. Spurgle himself.

"Just act casual," whispered Joe.

"Don't I know you boys?" said Lamar J. Spurgle
(who never forgot a face).
"I don't think so," said Spud.

"We're from out of town," said Joe.
But before they could slip past,
something unfortunate occurred.

Intrepid got bored,
jumped out of Joe's satchel,

and landed on a nice, shiny spot.
"Egads!" cried Spurgle.

Joe tried to make a run for it.

But Lamar J. Spurgle was quick on the draw.

"Well, well, well," said Spurgle. "Well, well, well."

The boys didn't like *that* one little bit.

In his office,
Spurgle read the boys the riot act.
And he confiscated all their things.
"If there's one thing I can't *stand*,"
said Spurgle, "it's a cut-up!"
Spud and Joe promised
to be on their best behavior—
for the rest of their lives.

Unfortunately, some habits are hard to break.
"He'll never catch us," said Spud.

But Lamar J. Spurgle just seemed to have
the knack.
"Think again, boys," said Spurgle.

During morning recess Spud and Joe were put to work washing Lamar J. Spurgle's repulsive dog, Bessie.

She was old and cranky,
and she had lots of bald patches.
"That guy really has it in for us," said Spud.

If it wasn't one thing, it was another.
"Put those comic books away this minute!"
boomed Spurgle.

"He's everywhere," whispered Joe.

During afternoon recess, they were able to relax.

Spurgle was nowhere to be seen.

"That guy is really cramping our style," said Spud.

Just then they heard a loud car radio.

"St. Bridget's got out early," said Mary Frances.
"And I have some time to kill.
Would you like to go for a little spin?"

"You bet!" cried Spud and Joe.
And they piled into Mary Frances' car.

"Step on it!" cried Joe.

But they didn't get far.

"I hereby confiscate this car!" said Spurgle.

"It is on school property,
and now it's mine."

"Holy smoke!" said Spud.
"Old man Spurgle's got your car now,
and he'll *never* give it back!"

"We'll see about that," said Mary Frances.
And she went to make a telephone call.

"Sometimes you just have to know when to get help," she said.

"She's calling the cops!" cried Spud.

"Better than that," said Mary Frances.
And in a few minutes, help had arrived.

Sister Aloysius of St. Bridget's
stepped out of the taxi cab.
"This will only take a minute," she told the driver.

Mary Frances explained what had happened.
"Step aside," said Sister.

And she dealt directly with the situation.

"Egads!" cried Spurgle.

"Return this car, *immediately*," said Sister.

"No, no, no," said Spurgle. "It's mine now."

Then Sister put on her glasses.

"Don't I know you?" said Sister Aloysius.

"Er," said Spurgle, "I don't think so."

"I've got it," said Sister.

"You're that Spurgle kid.

I taught you in grade school."

Spud, Joe, and Mary Frances were all ears.

"Lamar J. Spurgle went to *grade school*?"

whispered Joe.

"You were always taking other kids' things,"

said Sister to Spurgle.

"And you're still at it, I see. Shame on you."

"But—but," said Spurgle.

"Nobody messes with Big Al,"

whispered Mary Frances.

Just then Spurgle remembered a previous engagement.
"Take your old car," he said.
And he went inside.

"They haven't heard the last of Lamar J. Spurgle,"
he muttered under his breath.

Mary Frances was about to get into her car.
"Not so fast, dear," said Sister Aloysius.
And she got into the car herself.

"I could use a little spin," she said. "Gangway!"
"Wow!" said Joe. "Look at her go!"

"And how was your first day back at school?"
said Spud's mom.
"Oh," said Spud, "we're zipping right along."
But somehow Mrs. Jenkins didn't like the sound of *that*
one little bit.

El tesoro del tiburón

16

Escrito por Nyno Vargas
Ilustrado por Tony Griego

Un tiburón nada por el mar.

Ve un cofre entre los corales.

¿Será un tesoro? ¿Un tesoro de oro?

El tiburón jala la cuerda del cofre.

Pero no lo puede abrir.

¿Quién le puede ayudar?

Una tortuga se pasea por la arena.

—¿Me puedes ayudar? —dice el

tiburón—. ¡Es un tesoro!

El tiburón jala. La tortuga jala.

Pero el tesoro no sale.

—No puedo más —dice la tortuga con
la cara colorada.

Un loro se pasea por la arena.

—¿Nos puedes ayudar? —dice el

tiburón—. ¡Es un tesoro!

El tiburón jala. La tortuga jala. El loro jala.
Pero el tesoro no sale.

—No puedo más —dice el loro con

la cara colorada.

Una mariposa vuela por la arena.

—¿Nos puedes ayudar? —dice el

tiburón—. ¡Es un tesoro!

El tiburón jala. La tortuga jala.

El loro jala. La mariposa jala.

Todos jalan la cuerda.

¡Por fin sale el cofre!

En el cofre no hay oro.

—¿No hay tesoro? —dice el loro.

—¡En el cofre no hay oro, pero encontré
un tesoro! —dice el tiburón—. Un amigo
es un tesoro que vale más que el oro.

—¡Yo soy tu amigo! —dice el loro.

—¡Yo soy tu amiga! —dice la tortuga.

—¡Yo soy tu amiga! —dice la mariposa.

—¡Mis amigos son mi tesoro!

Mis palabras

Rr

ra	re	ri	ro
cara	arena	mariposa	loro
colorada			oro
corales			pero
será			tesoro

Palabras del cuento: abrir, ayudar, jalar

ISBN 0-590-97056-9   Copyright © 1998 by Scholastic Inc.   All rights reserved.   Printed in the U.S.A.
2 3 4 5 6 7 8 9 10   33   03 02 01 00 99